The Tell-Me Tree

KAREN INGLIS lives in London, UK. She writes picture books, chapter books and middle grade fiction for ages 3-11. Her time travel adventure *The Secret Lake* for ages 8+ hit bestseller charts in the UK and USA in 2018-20 and has been enjoyed by over over 200,000 children.

Visit kareninglisauthor.com to learn about all of Karen's books and sign up for a free sample of *The Secret Lake*.

Visit kareninglisauthor.com/picturebooks to join her picture books newsletter and download free posters and colouring sheets.

ANNE SWIFT is an architect, illustrator, artist and all-round unstoppable creative. She grew up on a farm in South Africa, studied architecture in Cape Town and moved to England over 30 years ago. She spends her time between London, Wiltshire and Cape Town - and sailing in the Med.

Anne and Karen met when their boys were at school and they've been friends for 25 years.

PLEASE WRITE A REVIEW . . .

If you enjoy *The Tell-Me Tree*, please take a moment to leave a short review online. It will help other parents and children discover the story.

Thank you!

Well Said Press
www.wellsaidpress.com

Published by Well Said Press 2020
83 Castelnau, London, SW13 9RT, England
All rights reserved.
ISBN: 978-0-9954543-3-0

Text copyright © Karen Inglis 2020
Illustrations copyright © Anne Swift 2020
Art direction and design Rachel Lawston, www.lawstondesign.com

The Tell-Me Tree

Karen Inglis • Anne Swift

Hello, I am the Tell-Me Tree.

Why don't you come and sit by me?

Tell me your worries,

tell me your cares,

share your best dreams

or your scary
nightmares.

However you feel . . .

happy

sad

worried

confused

I'm here to listen. It's your story.
You choose . . .

Tell me in pictures . . .

Tell me out loud . . .

Write it all down . . .

Anything's allowed!

You can bring a friend . . .

. . . or a grown-up too

- I know they'd love
to hear from you!

A problem you share soon feels lighter.
Let's talk together - you'll feel much brighter!

And good news you share will make us all proud.
Don't be shy - shout it out loud!

Now, if you need me and I'm not there,
do not worry, don't despair!

Simply draw your own
Tell-Me Tree, ready to
listen, just like me!

But for now, you know that I am here, ready and waiting to lend an ear.

So turn the page to speak to me, your perfect listener, the Tell-Me Tree.

Hello, I am the
Tell-Me Tree.

Why don't you come
and sit by me?

Tell me your
worries, tell
me your cares.

Share your best dreams or
your scary nightmares . . .

How are you feeling today?

Happy

Proud

Excited

Thankful

Sad

Cross

Shy

Unwell

Lonely

Confused

Can you draw a picture of how you feel?

Write down a few words about
how you're feeling today.

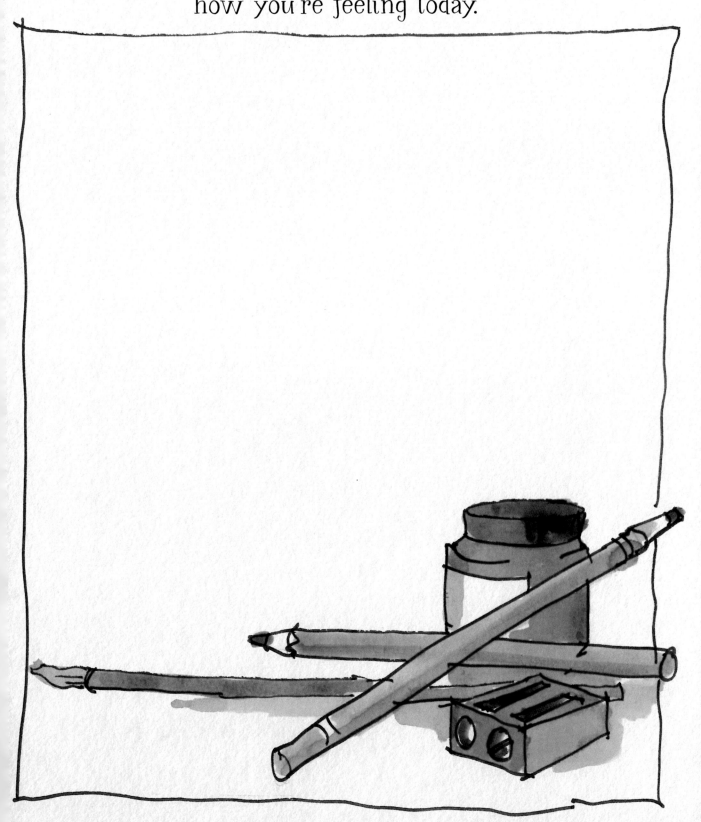

Who will you share your story with?

Can you draw a
picture of them?

Can you draw your own Tell-Me Tree?

See the last page for links to help you

Notes and links for grown-ups

Follow the link below to download a poster of the
Tell-Me Tree for use at home or in the classroom.

You'll also find tips and templates to help children draw their own
Tell-Me Tree, and factsheets about the wildlife on the last two pages.

kareninglisauthor.com/tellmetreeresources

Use the link below for resources on encouraging
children to talk about how they're feeling

kareninglisauthor.com/tellmetreeconversations

Made in the USA
Middletown, DE
25 February 2021